THE BEST OF SHOUT!

THE VOICE OF VICTORY FOR KIDS

ADVENTURE COMICS

THE BEST OF SHOUT! ADVENTURE COMICS

THE VOICE OF VICTORY FOR KIDS

All scripture is from the following translations:

The Holy Bible, New International Version © 1973, 1978, 1984 by the International Bible Society. Used by permission of Zondervan Publishing House.

International Children's Bible, New Century Version © 1986, 1988 by Word Publishing, Dallas, TX 75039. Used by permission.

The Best of *Shout!* Adventure Comics

ISBN-10 1-57562-251-3   30-1210
ISBN-13 978-1-57562-251-4

13 12 11 10 09 08   8 7 6 5 4 3

© 2000 Heirborne

Kenneth Copeland Ministries
Fort Worth, TX 76192-0001

Dear Comic Enthusiast,

When *Shout! The Voice of Victory for Kids* began in May 1994, our greatest desire was to create a magazine for kids that taught the uncompromised Word of God. In doing so, our first order of service was to decide what element would anchor the publication. While we realized short stories, activities and jokes would be part of the fun, it was unanimous that strong, Word-filled comics would accomplish our purpose.

Our three-man writing and drawing team turned out issue after issue, carefully combining exciting story lines and eye-catching graphics with the integrity of God's Word. Our prayer is that you enjoy each comic as much as we enjoyed producing them. Perhaps you will find, as we did, that *Wichita Slim* and *Commander Kellie and the Superkids*_{SM} become part of your world...and the Word they speak changes the way you look at it

The *Shout! The Voice of Victory for Kids* Staff

The Faith Adventures of WICHITA SLIM

The End

9

SHAUNA JUST RETURNED TO SHARE SOME EXCITING NEWS WITH HER FRIEND CLARA...

PSST! CLARA— CAN YOU KEEP A SECRET?

I GOT A BRAND NEW SILVER DOLLAR! I'M RICH! THINK OF ALL I CAN DO WITH IT!

WOW... WHERE'D YOU GET IT?

A NICE MAN GAVE IT TO ME—HE SAID HE WAS THE BANK...EXPLAINER...?

EXAMINER? THE BANK EXAMINER?

YEAH! ALL I HAVE TO DO IS UNLOCK THE BACK DOOR OF THE BANK BEFORE IT CLOSES, SO HE CAN INSPECT IT TONIGHT.

WHAT?!? THAT DOESN'T SOUND RIGHT.

C'MON, CLARA—I'LL TAKE YOU TO HIM. HE'S MY FRIEND.

YOUR FRIEND? I DOUBT IT. THIS IS TOO FISHY. THE BIBLE SAYS FRIENDS HELP EACH OTHER*—

IT SOUNDS LIKE HE'S TRYING TO GET YOU TO DO SOMETHING WRONG.

*PROVERBS 27:17

THERE HE IS!

WAIT! I DON'T THINK WE SHOULD GET ANY CLOSER— IT DOESN'T LOOK SAFE.

The End

13

The End

The End

17

The End

21

The End

23

"THE TOWN GOSSIP"

BILLY BOB STATLER ARRIVED IN TOWN JUST IN TIME FOR THE ANNUAL THANKSGIVING CELEBRATION...

HORSESHOES! PIE! TURKEY! I *LOVE* THIS TIME OF YEAR!

HEY, EVERYONE! HOW'S IT GOING?

CLINK!

???

WHA—WHY IS EVERYONE LEAVING?

BLUEBERRY PIE CONTEST!

OH, BOY! BLUEBERRY PIE!

READY...SET...

¡BLAM!

MUNCH! MUNCH! MUNCH!

MUNCH! MUNCH! MUNCH!

HUH?

HEY, THIS ISN'T FUNNY! WHERE'D EVERYONE GO?! I USE SOAP!

SMASH!

24

The End

25

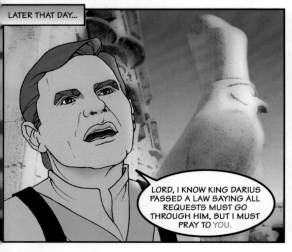

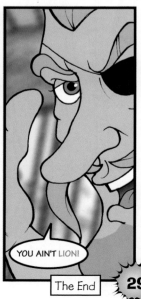

The End

29

PEEP!

HUH?!

GUESS GOD'S WORD IS MORE POWERFUL THAN YOUR DYNAMITE, DRAKE!

LET ME HAVE IT!

WHAT'D YOU DO?!

YOU CAN'T STEAL THE WORD, DRAKE—IT'S IN HIS HEART.

RRR...LOOKS LIKE THIS BANK DOESN'T HAVE ANYTHING I WANT...

WE'RE SAVED! AND SO IS ALL OUR MONEY!

I'LL LET SLIM KNOW WHAT HAPPENED. DRAKE WON'T BE ON THE STREETS FOR LONG.

AND WE HAVE SOMETHING MUCH MORE VALUABLE THAN MONEY...WE HAVE GOD'S PROMISES!

BIBLE

COOL.

The Faith Adventures of WICHITA SLIM

The End

33

The End

41

Plant—Just like you can put seeds into the ground, the Bible says you can plant God's Word and other good things into your own life and the lives of others! This is also called "sowing."

Harvest—When you plant sunflower seeds, you expect sunflowers to grow. In the same way, the Bible says when you plant something good into someone's life, afterward you will receive something good into your life (Ephesians 6:8)! If you plant food or clothes into someone's life, for example, that is what you will receive as well. Sometimes your harvest will come soon, and sometimes it will come later. This process is also called "reaping."

I received my harvest too!

The End

You can also be a **winner!** You can have an adventure just like Luis! In Galatians 6:7, God's Word says you'll harvest what you plant. That means you'll receive back the same thing you give to others in faith. If you plant seeds of love like he did, you'll get love in return. If you plant time, money or anything else, then *that's* what will come your way. So ask yourself, "What do I need from God?" and then plant that very thing!

SHOUT!
THE VOICE OF VICTORY FOR KIDS

Commander Kellie and the
SUPERKIDS
SK

"FIT FOR A DREAM" IN

ENJOYING THEIR DISCUSSION, COMMANDER KELLIE AND THE SUPERKIDS sm ARE UNAWARE OF WHAT'S HAPPENING NEARBY...

SO WHAT DO YOU ALL WANT TO BE WHEN YOU GROW UP?

MEANWHILE, IN ANOTHER PART OF THE ACADEMY...

THIS WILL PUT THE SUPERKIDS' PLANS ON HOLD!

TU KA!

UNTIL ALEX GROWS UP, HE'LL JUST HAVE TO KEEP ON DREAMING!

DREAM ON!

I'LL GIVE MYSELF 5 MINUTES TO GET OUTTA HERE...

TWINK

5:00

BZZZ

WITH GOD'S POWER WORKING IN HIM, GOD CAN DO MUCH, MUCH MORE THAN ANYTHING ALEX CAN ASK OR EVEN THINK!

EPHESIANS 3:20!

BYE-BYE SUPERKIDS!

THAT'S RIGHT, VAL—

COMMANDER KELLIE! MY SENSORS PICK UP THE HIGH-PITCHED VIBRATIONS OF AN ACTIVATED DETONATING DEVICE!

HA HA HA HA!

BEEP!

WHAT?!?

A BOMB!

4:48

The End

59

The End

67

"CAUGHT IN A BOTTLE"

RAPPER, CHECK THESE OUT!

THESE LETTERS REMIND ME OF A FEW WEEKS AGO WHEN YOU AND I RETURNED TO SECTOR 3 OF CENTRA CITY.*

DEAR COMMANDER KELLIE AND THE SUPERKIDS℠-

CAN YOU WRITE A STORY IN *SHOUT!* ABOUT KIDS DOING DRUGS? I SAY, "ONE THING YOU SHOULD DO IS OPEN THE BIBLE AND READ IT IF YOU FEEL LIKE YOU NEED DRUGS."

LOVE, MELODY CALIFORNIA

I WOULD LIKE TO SEE IN *SHOUT!* A STORY TO SHOW KIDS HOW TO SAY NO! TO DRUGS.

GOD BLESS YOU. STEPHANIE, AGE 12 TENNESSEE

I WOULD LIKE TO SEE A STORY ABOUT KIDS OVERCOMING DRUGS.

CHAKA SOUTH CAROLINA

YEAH, I REMEMBER TALKING TO RIKKI AND HIS GANG. THE NEXT THING I KNOW, YOU DISAPPEARED —WHERE DID YOU GO?

"WELL, YOU WERE TALKING TO RIKKI AND THE 'GUARDIAN ANGELS'..."

YOU'VE ALL SURE CHANGED FROM WHEN WE FIRST MET YOU.*

WE'VE COME A LONG WAY. BUT THERE ARE STILL A FEW "RED DEVILS" THAT HAVEN'T CHOSEN JESUS... WE'RE PRAYING FOR THEM.

*SEE ADVENTURE IN CENTRA CITY CASSETTE.

"...WHEN I SAW SOMETHING IN A NEARBY ALLEY."

CLINK!

WHA—

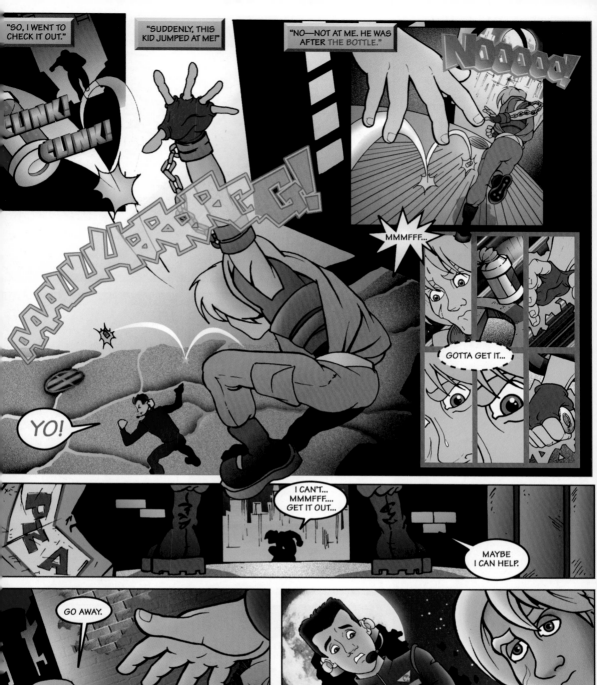

YOU KNOW, TO GET YOUR HAND OUT, YOU'LL HAVE TO LET GO OF THE BOTTLE.

YOU DON'T UNDERSTAND, KID. I'M NOT LETTING GO OF THIS BOTTLE. I HAVE TO HAVE IT.

BUT WHY—

IT'S DRUGS, ISN'T IT, TODD?

SO WHAT? YOU GONNA TELL ON ME, KID?!

WHHSOOM

THUM

GOD CAN SET YOU FREE, TODD.

I DON'T NEED TO BE SET FREE.

REALLY?

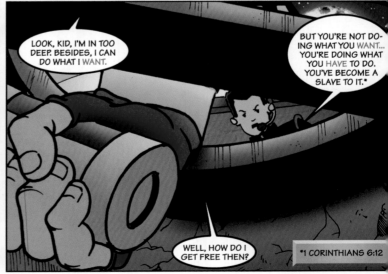

LOOK, KID, I'M IN TOO DEEP. BESIDES, I CAN DO WHAT I WANT.

BUT YOU'RE NOT DOING WHAT YOU WANT... YOU'RE DOING WHAT YOU HAVE TO DO. YOU'VE BECOME A SLAVE TO IT.*

WELL, HOW DO I GET FREE THEN?

*1 CORINTHIANS 6:12

*2 CORINTHIANS 5:17

The End

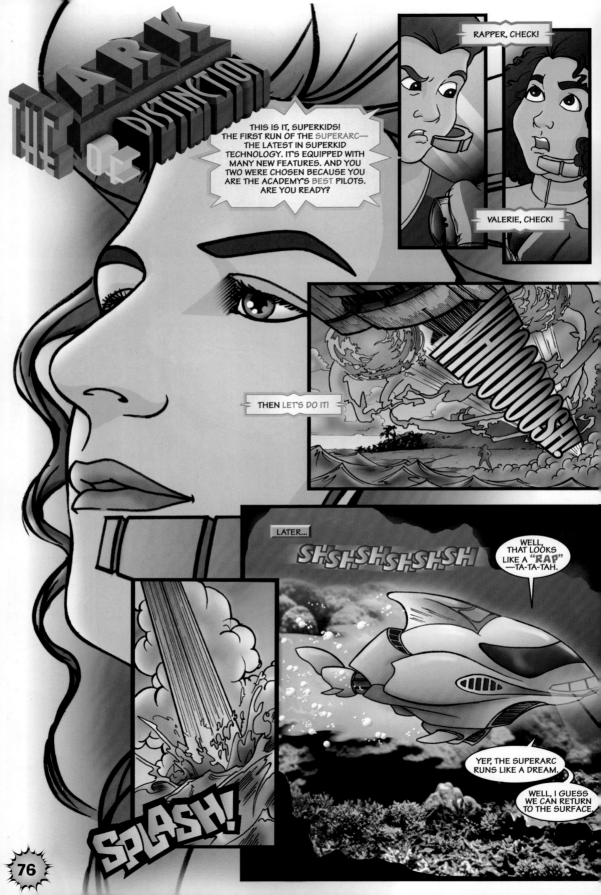

THE ARK OF DISTINCTION

THIS IS IT, SUPERKIDS! THE FIRST RUN OF THE SUPERARC— THE LATEST IN SUPERKID TECHNOLOGY. IT'S EQUIPPED WITH MANY NEW FEATURES. AND YOU TWO WERE CHOSEN BECAUSE YOU ARE THE ACADEMY'S BEST PILOTS. ARE YOU READY?

RAPPER, CHECK!

VALERIE, CHECK!

THEN LET'S DO IT!

WHOOOOOSH!

LATER...

SHSHSHSHSHSH

WELL, THAT LOOKS LIKE A "RAP" —TA-TA-TAH.

YEP, THE SUPERARC RUNS LIKE A DREAM.

WELL, I GUESS WE CAN RETURN TO THE SURFACE.

SPLASH!

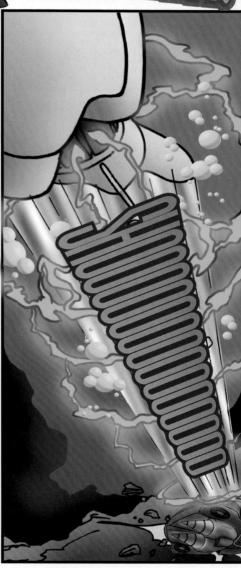

The End

"BREAKTHROUGH TO FREEDOM"

ALEX AND PAUL ARE ON THEIR WAY BACK TO SUPERKID ACADEMY AFTER COLLECTING FIREWOOD FOR CHRISTMAS EVE...

RRRUMMBLLE

RRRUMMBLLE

RRRRRUMMMMBLLLLE

VVVVMMMMMMMMM!

VVVVMMMMMMMMMMMM

HEY, PAUL, DO YOU HEAR SOMETHING?

ALEX! LOOK OUT!

WHOOOAA!

VVVVMMMMMMMMM!

ALEX QUICKLY HEADS INTO A NEARBY SNOW CAVE TO AVOID BEING OVERTAKEN BY THE AVALANCHE. BUT STRAIGHT AHEAD HE DIDN'T SEE...

THE CAVE WALL!

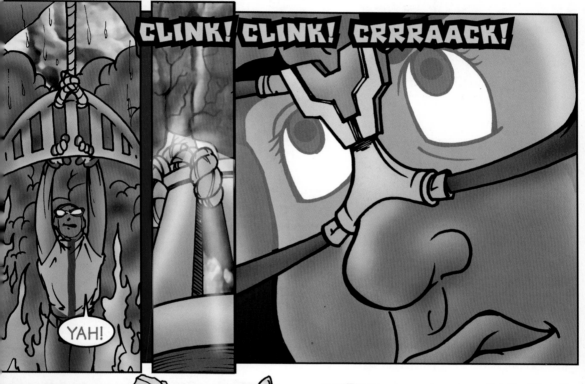

SUPERKIDS' MOTTO

All things are possible with God and we can do all things through Christ which gives us strength!

Luke 1:37 • Philippians 4:13

WORD WORDS

Angel—Angels are ministering spirits who serve God and are sent to help people (Hebrews 1:14). God has sent them to watch over you and protect you. You can instruct angels to protect you every day or help you when you need it.

Releasing Faith—Faith is a force on the inside of a Christian. It has the power to change things when you release it in a situation. It means choosing to believe "on purpose" God's Word, or that God is going to do something you've prayed for, instead of believing in what you see (2 Corinthians 5:7).

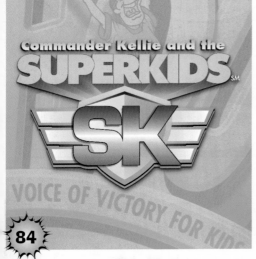

Commander Kellie and the SUPERKIDS℠

VOICE OF VICTORY FOR KIDS

IF YOU EVER NEED PROTECTION, YOU CAN PRAY GOD'S WORD, LIKE LEANNE DID! HERE'S A PRAYER BASED ON PSALM 91 THAT YOU CAN PRAY ANY TIME—

Father, I praise You that I can go to You, the God Most High, for safety. I will say to You, "Lord, You are my place of safety and protection. You are my God and I trust You." For You will save me from hidden traps and deadly diseases. Your truth will be my armor and shield. I will not fear any danger by night or by day. Nothing bad will happen to me. No disaster will come to my home. For You have put Your angels in charge of me to watch over me wherever I go. Yes, Lord, I love You and when I call to You, I know You will answer. You will be with me in trouble. You will save me, protect me, rescue me and honor me. You will give me a long, full life and I will see how You can save. Thank You, Father!

87

"TIME BOMB"

A SPECIAL SCENE FROM COMMANDER KELLIE AND THE SUPERKIDS.' NEW MOVIE, THE SWORD!

TODAY WE'RE GOING TO MEET SOMEONE. A NEW STUDENT-CADET NAMED C.J. IS TEMPORARILY JOINING THE BLUE SQUAD TO COMPLETE THE SUPERKID ACADEMY TRAINING.

SOMEONE NEW?!

IN THE BLUE SQUAD?

WE'VE NEVER HAD ANYONE NEW IN THE BLUE SQUAD.

I'M JUST NOW GETTING USED TO YOU GUYS...

WE CERTAINLY NEVER GET ANY NEW ROBOTS.

NOT SINCE WE WERE NEW CADETS.

COMMANDER DANA AND I DID A THOROUGH BACKGROUND CHECK AND THIS CANDIDATE HAS PERFORMED EXCEPTIONALLY IN ALL AREAS OF TRAINING,

TESTING AND ACCOUNTABILITY ANALYSIS.

BUT DOES C.J. KNOW THE WORD?

AS WELL AS ANY CADET IN THE ACADEMY.

JESUS ANSWERED: "WATCH OUT THAT NO ONE FOOLS YOU." MATTHEW 24:4

WORD WORDS

FEAR—THE OPPOSITE OF FAITH, FEAR IS BELIEVING ANYTHING THAT IS CONTRARY TO WHAT GOD'S WORD SAYS. IT IS DESIGNED FOR ONLY ONE PURPOSE: TO STOP YOUR FAITH AND MAKE YOU FAIL! WHEN FEAR ARISES, YOU CAN COMBAT IT AND WIN BY STIRRING UP YOUR FAITH. YOU DO THAT BY READING, SPEAKING AND PRAYING GOD'S WORD.

DREAD—ANOTHER WORD FOR FEAR.

DECEIVE—WHEN SOMEONE MISLEADS YOU TO BELIEVE SOMETHING IS TRUE, BUT IT IS REALLY A LIE. SATAN WILL TRY TO DECEIVE US INTO BELIEVING GOD'S WORD WON'T COME THROUGH FOR US...BUT THE TRUTH IS, IT WILL ALL THE TIME (HEBREWS 4:12-13).

89

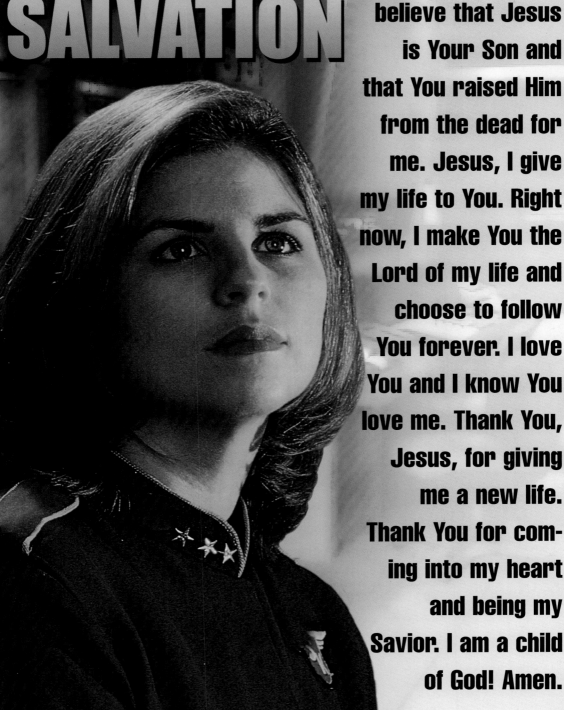

PRAYER OF SALVATION

Father God, I believe that Jesus is Your Son and that You raised Him from the dead for me. Jesus, I give my life to You. Right now, I make You the Lord of my life and choose to follow You forever. I love You and I know You love me. Thank You, Jesus, for giving me a new life. Thank You for coming into my heart and being my Savior. I am a child of God! Amen.

Other Books Available

And Jesus Healed Them All (confession book and CD gift package)

Baby Praise Board Book

Baby Praise Christmas Board Book

Load Up—A Youth Devotional

Noah's Ark Coloring Book

Over the Edge—A Youth Devotional

The Best of *Shout!* Adventure Comics

The *Shout!* Giant Flip Coloring Book

The *Shout!* Joke Book

The *Shout!* Super-Activity Book

Wichita Slim's Campfire Stories

*Commander Kellie and the Superkids*_{SM} **Books:**

The SWORD Adventure Book

*Commander Kellie and the Superkids*_{SM} Solve-It-Yourself Mysteries

*Commander Kellie and the Superkids*_{SM} Adventure Series:
Middle Grade Novels by Christopher P.N. Maselli:

#1 The Mysterious Presence

#2 The Quest for the Second Half

#3 Escape From Jungle Island

#4 In Pursuit of the Enemy

#5 Caged Rivalry

#6 Mystery of the Missing Junk

#7 Out of Breath

#8 The Year Mashela Stole Christmas

#9 False Identity

#10 The Runaway Mission

#11 The Knight-Time Rescue of Commander Kellie